GENTLEMAN BEAR

GENTLEMAN BEAR

#1907

WILLIAM PÈNE DU BOIS

FARRAR · STRAUS · GIROUX   NEW YORK

Copyright ©1985 by William Pène du Bois
All rights reserved
Library of Congress catalog card number: 84-48320
Published simultaneously in Canada by Collins Publishers, Toronto
Color separations by Offset Separations Corp.
Printed in the United States of America
by Rae Publishing Company
Bound by A. Horowitz and Sons
Designed by Atha Tehon
First edition, 1985

For
Harold and Irene Brooks-Baker,
their daughters Nadia and Natasha,
and the good bear Brown

mother, hopping

grand Champions Bentley and Lagonda

grandfather,
cheerfully refusing
to be interviewed

Father,
"Lord Boom-Boom"

1913

Lord Billy Browne-Browne is an Englishman who lives mostly in London. He has spent the biggest part of his life with a teddy bear. His bear's name is Bayard. Sir Billy is now sixty-eight years old. Bayard Bear is sixty-four. Sir Billy and Bayard are quite inseparable.

If style in behavior is handed down father-to-son, such a fellow probably had curious ancestors. Perhaps it started with his grandfather, Sir Malcolm Browne-Browne. Sir Malcolm Browne-Browne was born Sir Malcolm Browne. His name was changed from Browne to Browne-Browne when he entered the House of Lords. This was to distinguish him from a fellow Lord, Sir Ambrose Browne—no relation—in vote calls. There are barely enough names to go around in England.

Sir Malcolm was a famous cricketer. He rarely talked. Famous as he was, he never once let himself be interviewed. In the year 1950, when he was eighty-five years old, he was voted greatest batsman of the half century. After eating and drinking his way through a gala dinner in his honor, he unexpectedly stood up and said, "Gentlemen, if I had it all to do over again . . . .I'd jolly well do it!"

It was the shortest afterdinner speech of all time.

In a rare conversation with his son, Sir Peter Browne-Browne, Sir Malcolm confided, "I've never read, seen, or heard anything intelligent said by a sportsman. Please remember that, my boy."

Sir Peter did.

Sir Peter Browne-Browne was an internationally respected judge of pug dogs at dog shows. He was Billy's father. He always had at least two pug dogs of his own, and was quite unhappy when they were not at his feet. From time to time, he talked to them.

Once, late in life, he was approached by a man who remarked that he had always thought that pug dogs were ugly until he got one.

"Why did you get one?" Sir Peter asked, hoping to put a quick end to the conversation.

"Well," the man went on, "the late Duke of Windsor was a great pug fancier. I asked him why he liked pugs so much. Without a moment's hesitation, he replied, 'Pug dogs are darling puppies up to the age of three, then settle down to being adorable.' "

"Well put," Sir Peter mumbled. The rare times Sir Peter talked, his words hardly carried beyond his own necktie. He looked at his watch, smiled, and sped away.

Sir Peter Browne-Browne's wife, Lady Betty, once remarked to him, "You know, darling, I do believe you've spoken more to pug dogs than to all of the people we know combined."

"I'm certain you're right, dearest," said he.

There were rare times when Billy's father did speak up. One was in the month of May 1913, when he won Billy's mother at tennis in the Wimbledon championships.

In the winter of the same year, Sir Peter Browne-Browne entered a tournament in Pasadena, California. He had a technically sound, dull, and steady game. Things went well for him until he met an exciting American player known as the California Comet. The Comet had invented a new shot, the cannonball service. The Comet won nearly all of the games he served at love, leaving Sir Peter feeling sad and humiliated. Sir Peter was good at imitating people. He bought twelve dozen tennis balls and practiced the cannonball service four or more hours a day for two months. He couldn't wait to enter Wimbledon.

The borrowed serve worked well and attracted a great deal of attention. It was called "magnificent" by some players, "downright unfair" by others. Some irate tournament officials suggested that either the shot be forbidden, the net made higher, or the area in which a player serves made smaller. The press loved the fuss and nick-named him Lord Boom-Boom.

Lady Betty Wheatmill was another revelation at the 1913 Wimbledon tournament. She was a pretty girl with a freckled face and carrot hair set off by a sailor dress and a straw hat trimmed with pale blue ribbon. She returned every shot no matter how hard it was hit at or away from her, and always smiled cheerfully. The sports reporters loved her. They nicknamed her Little Lady Knock-It-Back.

Sir Peter couldn't keep his eyes off Lady Betty and watched every match of hers. Lady Betty, too, seemed somewhat fascinated by Sir Peter. Lady Betty was the first girl player to hop around between shots. This helped her to be in the right position to stroke the ball back.

In the finals, Lady Betty Wheatmill met Molly Molloy, an old-timer with a gruff face and a husky voice. Miss Molloy couldn't stand the smiling Lady Betty, who was hopping up and down and beating her.

She complained to the referee about—of all things—Lady Betty's hat ribbon. "All I can see is that silly ribbon flying all over her head. How can I keep my eye on the ball?"

Without saying a word, Lady Betty produced a pair of scissors at courtside, cut the ribbon off, and presented it to Molly Molloy.

Sir Peter Browne-Browne, watching the match from the stands, jumped to his feet, clapped, then roared with laughter. The idea of a winner presenting a loser with a blue ribbon was to him the most stylish gesture he'd ever seen.

Sir Peter, in his finals, was having an easy afternoon against Joe Sayres when, after a short talk as the players changed sides, his game seemed to fall apart. They changed sides again, again Joe Sayres spoke to him, and thereafter Sir Peter's game collapsed.

What Joe had said the first time was: "I hope you've polished up your dance steps for the opening victory dance. You know, of course, that at the Wimbledon Victory Ball the men's winner is out there, *all alone*, with the girls' winner?"

The second time, he'd said, "If you haven't prepared a *decent speech* for the Wimbledon Victory Ball, I might sell you mine. My wife found it rather comical."

Having won the first two sets, Sir Peter quickly lost the third and fourth. Then a beautiful smile lit up his face, his eyes shone bright, and he boom-boomed his way to easy victory.

What had happened was this: After being terrified with the idea of the first dance and the speech, he suddenly remembered that Lady Betty Wheatmill was the girls' champion, and that he'd be out there *all alone* with her. His fear vanished.

At the Wimbledon Victory Ball, out there all alone with Lady Betty Wheatmill, Sir Peter Browne-Browne quite lost himself and danced the most exuberant bunny hug ever seen.

"If you can slow down for a second," Lady Betty shouted, "I'll make you a bet."

"What's the bet?" Sir Peter roared.

"I'll bet you anything you want I can return five out of ten of your cannonball serves."

"You're on!" Sir Peter shouted, kissing Lady Betty.

Sir Peter Browne-Browne's speech took care of itself. "Ladies and gentlemen," he said, squeezing Lady Betty's hand, "we two have just made a lovely bet. Lady Betty Wheatmill says that she can return five out of ten of my cannonball serves. I say she cannot. The bet is that I shall gladly marry her if she can. And, of course, she *must* marry me if she cannot!"

People who rarely speak are liable at times to act with an impulsive lack of control.

"See you all tomorrow, ten o'clock, center court!" He made an elaborate bow.

Lady Betty's speech was even briefer. Blushing and pushing Sir Peter away, she said, "That's not a fair bet at all, but I still say I *can*!"

Sir Peter and Lady Betty were married the next day without bothering to see who would win the bet. "We love each other much too much for anything to come between us," Lady Betty told her startled parents.

Sir Malcolm Browne-Browne was pleased and also surprised. He found it hard to imagine his son actually asking a girl to marry him. "Do you know, Peter," he said, "that thousands of people turned up at center court to see who would win the bet? It was quite naughty of you two not to show up."

"We saw the people," Peter said, "and we also saw at least fifty reporters. We thought of all those interviews, those impertinent questions, and ran away."

"Well done," said Sir Malcolm. Then, turning to Lady Betty, he said, "And she's such a pretty thing." Sir Malcolm wrapped his big arms around his new daughter-in-law and kissed her loudly on both cheeks.

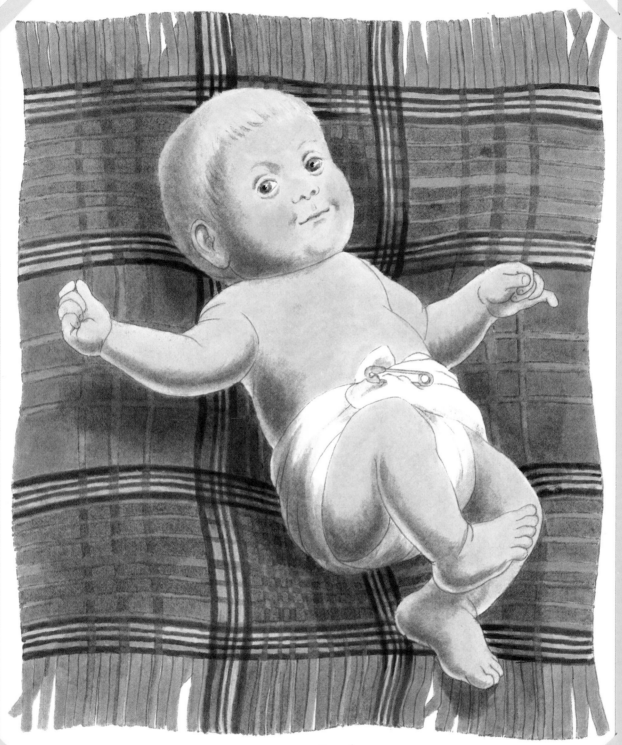

Billy, four months, on one of the pug's blankets

1916

On the ninth day of May 1916, a son was born to Lady Betty and Sir Peter Browne-Browne.

He was a lump of a child who weighed ten pounds and had wispy tufts of blond hair. His face was so fat that his eyes couldn't open for two whole days. When they did open, they were seen to be blue. Add apple cheeks to blond hair and blue eyes for a standard English baby boy.

Lady Betty wanted first to name him Buster Browne-Browne, after Buster Brown, the naughty funny-paper boy. This idea made Sir Malcolm howl, "When my grandson is paged in the barroom of Shepheard's Hotel in Cairo, I don't want him to be embarrassed by impertinent giggles!"

This exclamation, though exotic in thought, seemed to make perfect sense to Lady Betty and Sir Peter. Their son was christened William Browne-Browne, but he was always known as Billy.

When Billy was one week old, his father yanked him from his crib, took him to a table, stared deeply in his eyes, looked in his mouth, felt his shoulders, grabbed him by his thighs, rolled him over, picked him up, and returned him to his mother.

"Well, what do you think of him?" she asked with a big, proud smile.

"Head's too big, ears do not fold over," said Peter with great authority. "Legs aren't far enough apart, elbows too loose, toes not properly split up. His back arches a bit, he has no proper face wrinkles—"

"PETER!" Lady Betty screamed. "Our son is *not* a pug dog!"

Sir Peter smiled, kissed Lady Betty, and said, "Just teasing—he's a terribly handsome baby, darling."

When Billy Browne-Browne was born, World War I, the Great War as it was called, was at its fiercest. Sir Peter was chosen to work in the Censorship Bureau in London, where he spent the day on the telephone but never said a word.

Once an unfortunate fellow tried to install a telephone in Sir Peter's home. Sir Peter listened to him politely, then mumbled, "Do you mean that anyone, in any part of the world, can ring a bell in my home? Do you mean that, to make that bell stop ringing, I will have to speak to the impostor? Get out of my house."

A Browne-Browne never talked about the weather or a person's health. They were a private lot.

Sir Peter, as a child, once said to his father, Sir Malcolm, "Lovely day, isn't it, Father? How are you?" He had heard other people talk that way and was imitating them.

Sir Malcolm took his son by the shoulders, looked him sternly in the eyes, and said, "Peter my boy, the weather speaks quite clearly for itself. It does not need an interpreter. And that goes for such rubbish as 'How are you?' Gentlemen and ladies should never go around reminding each other that they are falling apart day by day."

Billy Browne-Browne was two when the horrible war ended. His father took him by the hand and they went for a walk together, late at night, long after Billy's bedtime. In the dark and quiet London streets they met another father with another boy of two taking a similar walk.

Both fathers burst into tears.

This was simply because peace had returned at last and they were all four lucky enough to be survivors.

No conversation was necessary to express their joy.

1920, Billy rolls again

1920

Billy Browne-Browne's head *was* too big for his body. Face to face, his head was round with fat cheeks, and from the side it was shaped like a Zeppelin with an ear in the middle. Once he learned how to walk, he never went downstairs without tripping and rolling all the way to the bottom. After much thought, his mother decided that if he carried something soft and stuffed it would cushion the roll. "I know!" cried Lady Betty. "I'll get him a teddy bear." Sir Peter approved immediately. "But I'll pick him out," he announced. He obviously considered himself to be the person best qualified to judge even a stuffed animal.

He went to the finest toy shop in London, where he was recognized by a saleslady who sat him down at a table covered with a green velvet cloth and produced four handsome specimens of teddy bears. She lined them up in a row facing Sir Peter, and proceeded to give each bear points for its qualities, exactly like a judge at a dog show.

"I would award these three ten out of ten points for straightness of back," she began. "The fourth seems to cave in at the shoulders. They all get ten points for coat. This one's eyes are positively dazzling, but this other has a whimsical expression considered desirable in the breed. This one's articulation is superb, but his sense of balance is a bit off. They all have well-rounded ears—ten each for ears. Paws and paw pads are fine. Which one do you prefer, Sir Peter?"

Sir Peter was deadly serious, giving each bear a thorough once-over. "They are all splendid," he said finally, "but I like the one with the dazzling eyes. He seems the most intelligent. I'll take him."

"Is this a gift, may I ask? I believe you have a boy."

"He'll be four tomorrow, but this isn't one of his birthday presents. He keeps rolling downstairs, flailing his arms around, getting himself all bruised . . ."

"I see," said the saleslady, who didn't see at all. "He does look intelligent." She slid him feet first into a bag and handed him to Sir Peter.

When Billy Browne-Browne met his bear, it was love at first sight. Then a sad thing happened. When he rolled downstairs with his new friend in his arms, a squeaker in the bear's tummy made loud grunt sounds from step to step. The idea that he was to blame for hurting his bear made Billy burst into tears. The next morning, when the two of them went downstairs again, Billy was careful, walked slowly, watched where he placed his feet, and held on to the banister. It took much more time, but they made it standing up, all the way down.

When Billy and his bear reached the last step, his father stood up and clapped his hands. "Happy birthday, Billy!" he shouted. "You are truly a grownup fellow. I shall take you to my tailor's tomorrow and have him make you some real sailor suits."

From that day on, Billy never again rolled downstairs.

After lunch the next day, Lady Betty appeared with a book of names. "We must name your bear, Billy," she said. "Is it a boy or a girl?"

)18

"He's a boy, of course!" Billy shouted.

"I was just asking," his mother said. She read names, and each time she suggested a new one, Billy looked directly into his bear's bright eyes, trying to see if the name fitted. "There is Bambalino, which means little baby; Bayard, a gentleman of courage and honor; Blyth, a happy chap; Bruno means brown; Helmut, famous, courageous; Philibert, very bright; Sylvester, a wood dweller—"

"Stop—we like Bayard best," Billy said. "Bayard Bear."

"I do, too," his father said, then added, with a faraway look in his eye, "When he's paged in the barroom of Shepheard's Hotel in Cairo, we wouldn't want him to be embarrassed by impertinent giggles, would we?"

"What on earth would Bayard Bear be doing in the barroom of Shepheard's Hotel in Cairo?" Billy's mother asked.

"Having a cub sandwich, perhaps," Sir Peter mumbled. "Come on, Billy, we're off to my tailor's."

First tailor-made suits

1920

"Billy, you're not taking Bayard to my tailor's, are you?"

"I can't leave him home, he'd have no one to talk to. And, besides, he wants to go."

"Does he talk so much?"

"Yes, he does. Yesterday, when we were opening my birthday presents together, he had something to say about every one of them."

"Did he like them?" Billy's father asked.

"Oh, he loved them all!"

"Well, that's good." They were leaving the house. "What's he saying now?"

"He says he was thinking of going back to the toy store to tell his old friend how happy he was, but he's afraid someone might try to keep him there."

"We won't go there, then."

They walked together up Regent Street, crossing the street before they reached Bayard's toy store, turning left at Princes Street and stepping into Wyser & Bryant's, Lord Peter Browne-Browne's tailors.

They entered a small room in the middle of which there was a table covered with books of suiting samples. There were tall mirrors in three corners of the room, and a scale of some sort in the fourth, with a leather chair sitting in it. "What's that for?" Billy asked shyly.

"That's for weighing jockeys," the tailor explained.

Billy mumbled something to his father, which Sir Peter translated as: "He wants to know if he can weigh his bear in the jockey scale. He just got him the day before yesterday."

"Yes, of course," the tailor said. "We'll weigh the two of them together, then Billy without the bear, and figure the difference." It was found that Bayard weighed one pound and fourteen ounces.

Billy again mumbled something indistinct, which Sir Peter translated as: "He wants to know how tall his bear is." The tailor took a tape measure he had around his neck and measured Bayard. "He's a good, strapping twenty-two inches. Follow me," he said. He led Billy and his father into a dressing room.

The tailor stood Billy Browne-Browne on a table and measured him for four sailor suits, two summer ones in white, and two winter ones in navy blue. Each suit came with the traditional black silk necktie and a whistle attached to a braided white cord which went around the neck and tucked neatly into a breast pocket.

After the fitting, which took twice as long as it might have because Billy was so ticklish, Billy took his bear and stood him on the table. He pointed at Bayard and announced in a firm voice, "He's next!"

"What did your son say?" the tailor asked, somewhat abashed.

"Until today, he's never said much of anything . . ."

"I said Bayard's next," Billy Browne-Browne repeated. "He would like a summer suit in white and a winter suit in blue, same as mine, and he says please do not forget his whistles."

"I wouldn't think of it," said the tailor. On that day, Bayard Bear was fitted for the first two of over two hundred and fifty suits.

Leaving the tailor's, Billy stopped suddenly and said, "Bayard says he's hungry."

"What does he say he'd like to eat?"

"He was thinking of tea and ginger cookies at Fortnum & Mason's."

"Bayard has posh ideas," Billy's father offered.

When they got home, Billy's mother asked about the fitting. "It went well," Peter said, "and Billy actually had something to say this morning."

"What, for instance?"

"He ordered two sailor suits for Bayard Bear."

"And you, of course, agreed?"

"I didn't have a thing to say about it. He says Bayard wanted them. He says Bayard talks constantly and knows what he wants."

"Well, that's a change in the family! What does Bayard talk about?"

"Oh, all sorts of things," Billy's father mumbled. He turned and walked away.

grand old Hammer

1927, third Teddy-Bear-Six bash

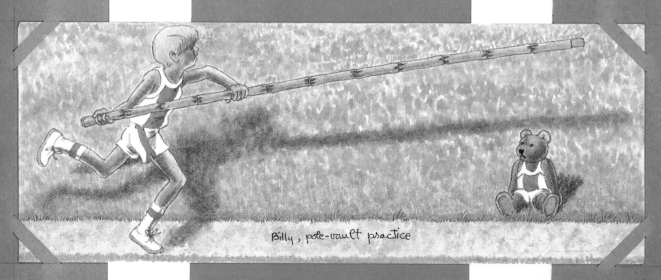

Billy, pole-vault practice

1924

Dressed identically in blue blazers, gray-flannel shorts, caps, red-and-white scarves, red-and-white ties, wool socks, and black shoes, Billy Browne-Browne and Bayard Bear were feeling sick with fear. They were about to be packed off to the Hammer School for Boys.

"We don't like this at all," Billy Browne-Browne muttered.

Billy's father knew exactly what his son was going through. "You'll like parts of it very much," Sir Peter said, trying hard to remember some one part of boarding school he liked.

"I loved tennis," his mother said, smiling and hopping up and down.

"Yes of course, tennis!" shouted Sir Peter.

"Bayard hates tennis!" Billy shouted back.

The drive to school, with a good two hours off at a warm and handsome inn, crackling with wood fires and smelling of roasting baby boar and beer, took place in four and a half hours of silence. Then up popped the Hammer School for Boys.

There it was, so big, red and white, banners flying, and spread out all over green lawns and playing fields.

"Well, what do you think of it?" Billy's father asked with some enthusiasm.

"I hate it!" Billy grumbled, squeezing Bayard so hard his tummy squeaker made a grunt sound for the first time in years. "See that?" he cried. "Bayard hates it, too!"

There was a short meeting in the Headmaster's office. Billy disappeared in a corner behind a high-backed chair.

"Our son is a shy boy," Lady Betty announced, "an only child."

The Headmaster was a tall man, comfortable and tweedy, but with a military bearing suggesting discipline. "So I see," said he, "but not to worry. I'm certain he'll get along."

An older boy popped into the office and pulled Billy by the hand out from behind the tall chair. He stood smartly at attention and asked, "Where to, sir?"

"C Dormitory in the East Wing," said the Headmaster.

Hugging Bayard tightly, Billy in turn was hugged by his mother and father before being marched off down a chilly hall. He turned in time to see the door close behind him as his parents waved and tossed kisses.

Once the door closed, the older boy let go of his hand. He had Billy's two suitcases—one large, the other toy-like, in matching leather. "What's in the little one?" he asked. "Your shaving stuff?"

"It's Bayard's clothes," Billy whispered in a soft whimper.

The older boy looked curiously at Billy, then spotted Bayard for the first time. "Oh, *that* Bayard," he said. "Well, you'll soon get over it." He spoke of the bear as though it were a case of the mumps.

At C Dormitory, Billy was turned over to a plump and motherly lady. "Miss Barstow," said the older boy, "this is Billy." He spun around and raced back, anxious to yank the next little boy from his parents' arms.

)26

"Well, at last we're all here," Miss Barstow announced. There were fourteen boys in C Dormitory. The East Wing had a long hall with big windows running down its length; fourteen beds stood in a row opposite them. The beds were separated by wardrobes, each with eight hangers and two drawers. Miss Barstow turned to Billy. "As you seem to be the shyest, I'll put you in the middle. That way, you'll quickly make friends." This sounded to Billy like telling an oversized boy that he was being put in the smallest cot to get used to being uncomfortable.

Then an odd thing happened which took Billy by surprise. Five boys quickly grabbed the beds on either side of his. Before he could figure this out, Miss Barstow again took over. "You all have the same things in your suitcases. I shall show you where each bit of clothing goes. Open your suitcases and do exactly as I do." The unpacking finished, she went to the door at the other end of the East Wing, pointed, and said, "This is the bathroom. You will find shower baths, toilets, and fourteen washstands in two rows of seven opposite each other. Each of you pick a basin, then have a washup before dinner. Off you go!" She left C Dormitory.

As soon as she had left, a tough-looking boy in a bed next to Billy's asked him in a whisper, "What's your bear's name?"

"Bayard," Billy whispered back.

"Where did he get the school uniform?"

"My dad's tailor made it, and my nanny made him socks and a scarf."

"Blimey, what a lucky bear!"

For the first time that afternoon, Billy grinned.

While the boys were washing up, Miss Barstow came back, snatched up Bayard Bear, and took him to the Headmaster's office.

"Sir, just look at what I found on Billy Browne-Browne's bed."

"It would seem to be a teddy bear. How old is the boy who owns it?"

"Eight years old."

"Rather old for a bear. He's the shy one, isn't he? Maybe his teddy will help to see him through hard times."

"Sir, may I be so bold as to ask you just what you mean by hard times? Our school is supposed to prepare boys for hard times."

Oddly enough, the Headmaster himself had a teddy bear in the den of his home, a bear which over the years had had his features loved right off his face. The Headmaster was not above asking the bear advice when problems arose.

"I was speaking of such hard times as homesickness, Miss Barstow, and—" At this point Billy Browne-Browne burst into the Headmaster's office. "Sir, my Bayard has been kidnapped!" he shouted.

The Headmaster stood to a fearsome height and said, "First of all, young man, boys do not burst into my office without knocking—boys do not come to my office at all without being summoned! Secondly, your bear is right here. You may keep him, but he must stay out of classrooms, study halls, dining rooms, and common rooms. That will be all."

"Thank you, sir," Billy said, turning beet-red and gingerly picking up Bayard. He tiptoed out of the room, shutting the door without making a sound.

"What did you just see, Miss Barstow?" the Headmaster asked.

"I saw a naughty boy."

"Quite the opposite, Miss Barstow. Bears build character. I hardly saw the boy earlier. He was so shy he hid behind that chair. Compare that with what we just witnessed. I repeat, bears build character."

"Rubbish!" said Miss Barstow.

Later on, in what seemed to be the middle of the night, Billy

Browne-Browne was awakened by the sound of suitcase locks clicking, followed by whispered conversations. He was too sleepy to figure it out, and besides, it was like part of a dream.

In the morning, he saw that the five boys in the beds nearest to his each had a teddy bear of his own. There was a fat boy whose bear was wearing pajamas with feet; a skinny boy whose bear was wearing silk boxing shorts, gloves, and shoes. The tough boy who had asked about Bayard's school uniform owned a bear who wore nothing at all. There was an East Indian boy whose bear wore a white outfit with tight trousers and turban. The fifth boy's bear was wearing the splendid uniform of the Coldstream Guards. At once these boys knew they needed each other almost as much as their bears. Soon they were known throughout the school as the Teddy-Bear Six.

Billy Browne-Browne's school days passed without event. Bayard was there for company and conversation, and the Teddy-Bear Six helped each other over the bigger bumps. Billy had all the friends he needed.

For sport he picked the pole vault. It was not a popular track event, and he and Bayard could spend afternoons left very much to themselves. Billy secretly wanted to go higher than anyone else in school, even just a jump, and with Bayard's help and backing, he was sure he could do it. He refused help from the coach. He was ashamed of himself when he found, after long afternoons of practice, that he could jump higher without the pole than with it. He looked Bayard desperately in the eyes and screamed, "We aren't getting anywhere!" The coach came running to his aid. "Before I leave you two alone again," he said, "I'll give you some sound, basic tips, both in vaulting and in training. You seem to have the desire." With the help of the coach's tips, Billy quickly doubled his previous efforts. He thanked Bayard for his constant support. His sixth year, he broke the Hammer

School pole-vault record, and Sir Peter invited the Teddy-Bear Six to his country home for a loud, fantastic bash.

His last year at school, Billy broke his earlier record by a full three feet, a vault which still stands unchallenged at Hammer. It enabled Billy Browne-Browne and Bayard Bear to coast through Oxford University as minor heroes. And it led right up to places on the British team for the Olympic Games of 1936, which were held in Berlin.

1936

Olympic Games waste a day in opening ceremonies. They include the lighting of a gigantic flame, followed by the release of thousands of doves all flying in one direction, then back again, vanishing with a thrashing of flapping wings. Then come thousands of robot gymnasts who transform the field into a huge piece of brightly colored cloth with zippers which open and shut at regular intervals. After the doves and robots comes the parade of teams from all nations in alphabetical order, Abyssinia to Zambia. Some countries send a flag and four or five athletes. Others send armies.

Dressed in blue blazer suits piped in red and white, Billy Browne-Browne and Bayard Bear marched in with the British team. Bayard was difficult to see because he was tucked under Billy's blazer. This made Billy look curiously lumpy for an athlete, but gave Bayard a chance to enjoy the pomp and ceremony of opening-day parade.

The parade serves two purposes. It gives the athletes the feel of the track beneath their feet, and the incredible sight and sound of an audience of one hundred thousand spectators. Normally, Billy and Bayard would have run far from such a terrifying scene, but Billy had acquired the singular poise which comes with long and careful training. He also still had that odd desire he first felt at Hammer when he took up pole vaulting, a wish to go higher than anyone else in a discipline which he had worked out mostly by himself. Shy people often have such fantasies.

After the pageantry Adolf Hitler, the host of the 1936 Olympics, announced that the games might begin. This was the signal for everyone to get up and leave. Nothing serious starts on opening day.

The pole-vault event didn't take place until the fourth day, an interminable wait for Billy and Bayard. Then suddenly they were out in the blazing sun, and Billy unzipped Bayard's warm-up suit and tucked the bear into his own crumpled suit in a place next to the pole vaulters' running path where he could watch the jumps.

There is nothing as exciting to a pole vaulter as the explosive sound of one hundred thousand people when he just barely clears the bar. Billy was in such a fever of concentration he paid little attention as the bar rose higher after each jump. Soon he was one of the last four competing for the medals, and he had actually jumped a full three inches higher than ever before. Now the bar was up still another inch. He missed his first two chances. There was only one left. He walked determinedly to where Bayard was sitting, plucked him from the warm-up suit, and sat him on the far edge of the huge pillow pole vaulters land in to break their fall.

He walked back up the running path, turned, lined up his pole, stared at the bar and the slot into which a vaulter sticks the end of his pole, stared into Bayard's bright eyes. *"Okay, Bayard, this is it!"* He thundered down the running path, up he went, feet over head, neatly clearing the bar and coming down *Whooosh!* in the landing cushion. At that exact moment Bayard Bear flew up in the air and back over the bar, catapulted by Billy's landing. He cleared it by at least two feet,

)32

When Billy landed, Bayard was catapulted high over the bar

and came down into the outstretched arms of Billy, who had scrambled back to cushion his fall. First thunderous laughter, then applause greeted this unexpected performance. Although Billy jumped no higher that afternoon, his last successful jump had earned him the third-place medal.

As host of the Berlin games, Adolf Hitler was thoroughly un-sportsmanlike. He had the overblown idea that if he chose to shake hands with a winning athlete, his handshake was every bit as good as a gold medal.

Outrage was his style.

He took joy in snubbing heroes.

Shock was the thing.

After the pole-vault event, Adolf Hitler approached the podium where the three winners stood. They had already received their medals. Adolf Hitler shook hands with the gold-medal winner, the Olympic pole-vault champion of 1936. Adolf Hitler shook hands with the runner-up, the silver-medal winner. Adolf Hitler then stood in front of Billy Browne-Browne, who had Bayard Bear in his arms. He looked from one to the other, Billy to Bayard, Bayard to Billy. Finally, in the stony silence, an evil, sarcastic grin split Adolf Hitler's face. He clicked his heels and shook hands with Bayard.

Gales of boisterous laughter rewarded this display of clown-like buffoonery.

Billy Browne-Browne was oblivious to the whole scene. After he had received his medal, he started daydreaming of quite another thing. He was planning to break training that evening, at a private dinner celebration with Bayard at the best restaurant in Berlin.

The flags of all nations which decorated the stadium produced visions of food and wine. The two of them were going to have caviar from Persia with vodka from Russia, a Dover sole from dear old

England with champagne from France. Next would be venison from Germany with braised endives from Belgium and a fine Italian wine. Then a selection of Dutch cheeses, before attacking pastry from Austria. Turkish coffee, of course, with an iced Danish aquavit. He could hardly wait. "Bayard adores restaurants," he mumbled to no one.

You cannot beat a true athlete for self-discipline, or beat him to the place in which he's chosen to break training.

BAYARD

der
Wunder-Bär

Avis yanked Bayard out
from under Billy's blazer
and kissed him on
the nose.

Staggering away from the restaurant, Bayard Bear tucked under his blazer, Billy Browne-Browne reeled into a black, red, and white movie theater. Feeling stuffed, he was hypnotized by arrows designed to funnel customers off the sidewalk, through the lobby, into an orchestra seat. He sank deep in red velvet and fell sound asleep.

Sir Billy must have been snoring, because he found his arm being shaken by a girl in a red uniform with a long flashlight in her white-gloved hand. She was pointing to the screen and seemed to be suggesting in German that the normal thing to do was to open one's eyes. He looked up just in time to see himself, Bayard, and Adolf Hitler in the newsreel.

The sequence had a title: BAYARD, DER WUNDER-BÄR. Billy was astounded. "How did they know your name?" he asked Bayard out loud. Then, to his embarrassment, he saw how. The newsreel showed Billy's last successful jump, and saw him sitting Bayard on the landing cushion. It was a close-up shot, and Billy was talking out loud to Bayard, "Come on, old chap, come on, dear old Bayard. I just know we'll make it this time. Sit here, Bayard, and I won't let you down. Now is when it all adds up, here is where we put it all together! *Okay,*

Bayard, this is it!" There were German subtitles under the action. The entire audience around him was thundering with laughter. Billy felt compelled to assure Bayard that everything was all right, but, nonetheless, slunk low in his seat. The film showed Billy clearing the bar, thumping in the cushion, catapulting Bayard. It showed the bear's somersaults back over the bar, and Billy slithering across the cushion to catch Bayard in his arms. The audience rose, laughing and applauding, and Billy sat back up straight. They repeated his and Bayard's jumps in slow motion, not once, but twice, each time to wild applause. The sequence ended with the podium scene, with Adolf Hitler shaking hands with Bayard, and Billy looking skyward from one flag to another.

Everyone loved Hitler's performance, but whistled loudly—which is the German way of booing—when a close-up of Billy's face showed him looking over Adolf Hitler's head, paying no attention whatsoever.

"I don't remember that at all," Billy told Bayard. The cameraman then walked around behind Billy to locate what in the sky could possibly be more interesting than Adolf Hitler. Could it be a British or French flag? "Oh, now I remember," Billy told Bayard. "Dover sole and champagne." He belched. "Excuse me, Bayard, perhaps we'd better leave."

In the lobby he noticed an extremely pretty girl staring in his direction. He quickly looked over his shoulder, hoping she was eyeing someone else. But no, he was quite alone.

"Excuse me," the girl said, "this is very rude, but I can't help saying how much I enjoyed your jump. And I find Bayard irresistible!"

"Oh, thank you," Billy said. "Bayard is now safely tucked away in bed, ha-ha."

"I've been seeing movies at different theaters all day," the girl continued. "I saw the newsreel clips of you and Bayard four times. I practically understand German now." She didn't mention that she, too, was in the newsreels.

"You look vaguely familiar—who are you?" Billy asked stupidly.

"Well, for one thing, it's obvious I'm on the same team you're on. Otherwise, I don't think we'd both be wearing these silly blazers."

"Oh, heavens!" Billy gasped. "You're Avis Allison, the diver. You won the silver medal today. I didn't recognize you with your clothes on. You were fantastic!"

"Do you have a swimming pool, Billy?"

"I'm about to build one. Actually, diving is part of my regular training." He stopped short, wondering why he had told two bold-faced lies in a row, and why his heart was thumping.

Avis Allison looked at her watch. "Good grief," she said, "it's nine forty-five. I must get back to camp before they set loose the blood-hounds."

"Oh, me too!" he shouted, immediately wondering why he was shouting. He decided then and there that he loved Avis Allison. He hadn't wanted to sound as though he was anxious to get away.

"May I kiss you good night?" Avis Allison asked.

"I suppose so, of course." It was the most incredible question anyone had ever asked him.

Avis Allison reached under Billy Browne-Browne's blazer, pulled out Bayard Bear, and kissed him smack on the nose.

1938

Later that evening, Avis Allison decided quite spontaneously that she must marry Billy Browne-Browne. This was a rash decision based entirely on intuition. It was an interesting challenge. It struck her that if she were to marry Billy she would have to do it all on her own, and make all the advances.

Meeting Billy in the grandstand the next morning, she took him by both hands, looked deep into his eyes, and said, "I've thought a great deal about our meeting last night, about how much we admired each other, about how we both have the same good taste in clothes, about our having similar interests such as sports and our fondness for Bayard, of how important all of these things are if a marriage is to work. Having slept on it, I find I agree with what you said with all my heart." Having delivered this embellished version of an altogether different conversation, she let go of his hands and dashed off to find a seat in the stands.

Billy Browne-Browne found himself standing red-faced, but extraordinarily pleased with himself. It was time to consult Bayard. "Did I really say that, Bayard?" he asked; then an odd feeling of terror came over him. In the past twenty-four hours he had been snubbed by Adolf Hitler and hadn't even noticed it, and he had proposed to a lovely girl without remembering that either. "The important thing, Bayard, is that I do believe that adorable girl likes us both very much." He sauntered off for a seat in the stands, searching the crowd for Avis Allison. He saw her a few rows down, closely guarding the seats on either side of her.

"Are those seats for us?" he asked, bounding to her side.

"Of course they are."

They watched the games, with Avis supplying an occasional running commentary. Billy peeked at her a lot but never said a word. She looked more and more desirable, a girl custom-made for himself and Bayard. He was trying desperately to compose a suitable little speech, but felt sure he had forgotten how to talk. Finally, when everybody else was getting up to leave, he shyly put his arm around her waist. "Yes, I will, and I cannot think of anything lovelier in the entire universe," he stammered.

It was doubtless the clumsiest marriage proposal of all time.

Avis Allison then proved that she was the only possible wife for Billy Browne-Browne. "I do, too," she said.

He invited Avis and Bayard to a perfectly silent dinner during which they both did a great deal of smiling and staring at each other. They ate what the headwaiter suggested and nodded when they both found they liked everything served. It seemed to be a choice rare evening to Billy, a dinner complete with exquisite conversation. Such is the magic of imagination. Avis Allison loved it, too. Bayard never stopped smiling. At nine-thirty, they separated to rush back to their dormitories, which were situated at opposite ends of Berlin.

Billy Browne-Browne found a cable from his father on his bed, saying: "Mother and I are terribly proud of you and Bayard. We saw your incredible jumps in the newsreels. Name any present you would like and it is yours. Love, Mother and Dad."

"I would like a swimming pool with a high diving board," Billy cabled back.

"How odd," Lady Betty exclaimed, after reading the cable. "Billy hates the water and can't swim."

Returning home to England, Billy found another cable, this one from California, U.S.A., which read: "Newsreel clips shown here have made you and Bayard the most popular athletes of the 1936 Olympic Games. May I please interview you? Name time and place." It was the first of many cables he was to get from America, all signed Richard Marshall. Billy read the cable to Bayard before crumpling it up and tossing it away. "This would make Grandfather Malcolm roar!" he told Bayard.

The second of June 1938, when the swimming pool on the rolling lawns of the Browne-Browne estate was first filled with water, Billy and Avis were married. The tent on the lawn beside the pool was in Wimbledon stripes of green and purple. The food was flown over from Paris. Ray Noble furnished the music.

Bayard was the best man, and he and Billy wore impeccably tailored cutaways.

The five other members of the Teddy-Bear Six arrived together, elegantly attired except for bright red-and-white Hammer School ties. They left their bears home so as not to steal one bit of Bayard's pleasure on this great day.

The bride looked positively adorable in a tiered and pleated crisp dress by Molyneux. Her great train was held by little Lady Pamela and little Lord Malcolm. They had been asked not to let go of it until told. They followed the bride right up to the end of the highest diving board, where Avis Allison inaugurated the pool with a perfect swan

)42

Followed faithfully by little Lady Pamela and
Lord Malcolm, Avis Browne-Browne dove into her new pool.

dive which made a tiny splash in the pool but big waves in every newspaper and magazine in the world.

The Teddy-Bear Six then pushed Billy Browne-Browne and Bayard into the pool. Billy let out a great howl before sinking like a stone to the bottom. Those who had pushed him then jumped in to save his life. Bayard Bear floated to the surface on his back. When rescued, he weighed ten pounds more than before his swim. It would take him two whole weeks to dry out thoroughly, somewhere near the ovens, in the kitchen.

Sir Billy and Lady Avis took the Orient Express to Venice that evening. Bayard stayed home.

Weeks later, at a Teddy-Bear Six bash in London, Billy Browne-Browne asked the others how they possibly could have been so heartless as to do what they had done to him and Bayard on his wedding day.

"We thought that Lady Avis would be just as happy without Bayard on her honeymoon, you silly fool!"

"Oh?" Billy said, rather wistfully.

"And since you never let go of him, you both ended up in the pool."

"Perhaps you were right. Anyway, thanks for the thought," said Billy, leading them off to the bar.

If this was what friends were all about, he was just as happy not to have bothered collecting more.

1944

While at Oxford together, one of the Teddy-Bear Six tried to convince the others that learning to fly was "as important to a gentleman as learning to sit on a bar stool. And less dangerous." They were a difficult lot to persuade. The others seemed just as happy to risk their lives behind a few beers as up in the clouds.

At an RAF-sponsored Air Club near Oxford, the Teddy-Bear Six met an enthusiastic old coot, suited up, goggled, and leather-helmeted in a World War I Air Pilot panoply. He romantically extolled the ecstasy of flying and won them over to a man. It would seem unfair to note that the seduction took place on the Air Club's bar stools.

In 1939, when war was declared, Billy Browne-Browne immediately enlisted in the RAF. After two months of extensive training, he found himself attached to a Spitfire squadron in southern England, as an officer pilot. In the hastily erected Quonset hut labeled C Barracks were the other members of the Teddy-Bear Six. Laughing at their good fortune to be together again, shaking hands and slapping backs, they clicked open suitcases in unison and out came six teddy bears. At this exact choice moment, Squadron Commander Carstairs entered C Barracks to greet his new pilots. The Teddy-Bear Six snapped to attention.

"At ease, men," said Commander Carstairs. He passed in review the Teddy-Bear Six. He was just about to give the traditional officer's speech of welcome, something along the lines of "Do everything I say correctly, immediately, and with a smile, night or day, and we cannot fail to get along," when he spotted six teddy bears in a row on six bed pillows. *"Mother save us!"* he howled. He turned, seemed about to leave, then reeled around to face the Teddy-Bear Six. "If I may, gentlemen, I will change somewhat what I was about to say . . . oh, I give up! You may keep those things, but I don't want to find them anywhere else on this base!"

The Teddy-Bear Six made good pilots who from time to time distinguished themselves in combat. More importantly, they managed to survive. Then, at a briefing one morning in the spring of 1944, Commander Carstairs marched in looking very grave indeed. "Something grim and evil is happening on the opposite banks of the Channel," he announced. "Strange ramps are being built. We've tried to photograph them but they're protected by radar, searchlights, and masses of antiaircraft fire. We must get intelligence photographs. I wouldn't dare tell you the number of planes lost so far trying to get them. Has any one of you chaps a brilliant suggestion to offer? Try for once to think before you speak!"

In the silence which followed, Captain Billy Browne-Browne remembered something his father had confided to him in London. It had to do with something Rolls-Royce was up to. "I wouldn't spread it around," his father had said, "although it's not that big a secret." Sir Peter Browne-Browne was back in Censorship.

Captain Billy Browne-Browne stood up.

)46

"Quiet, everyone!" shouted Commander Carstairs. "The silent Captain Billy is about to speak!"

"I've heard, sir," Billy mumbled bravely, "that Rolls-Royce has produced a dozen Sparrow engines, like the Merlin engines in our Spitfires, only half-sized. The engines have been mounted in twelve half-sized Spitfires with fuselages, wings, and tail assemblies made of wood to counter radar. These tiny new planes are called Sparklers. Now, sir, if we could procure six of these Sparklers, the Teddy-Bear Six could take a quick run at those ramps, shoot some pictures, turn, and head for home. My thinking is this: the enemy would see six familiar Spitfires heading their way and, being used to their size, shape, and sound, would hold fire until they came well within eye-and-ear range. The fact is, we would already be well within range and taking pictures."

Captain Billy sat down.

Commander Carstairs looked positively dumbfounded. He sternly eyed Captain Billy Browne-Browne. "Is this a plan to get yourself a week's rest in London?" he growled. "Are you simulating battle fatigue?"

"Not a bit, sir."

"Well, in that case, I'll give you exactly three days to come up with six 'Sparklers.' But look out! They'd better exist!"

The Sparklers were produced, and the Teddy-Bear Six set out immediately to prepare them for the mission. They were found to be slower than hoped for, nowhere near as fast as any German fighter plane. This meant that, if they were chased on their way to the mission or heading back to base, they would have to pretend to have been hit and simulate crashing. And pilots must somehow be seen bailing out.

Movie cameras were first loaded in the gun mounts. Then an

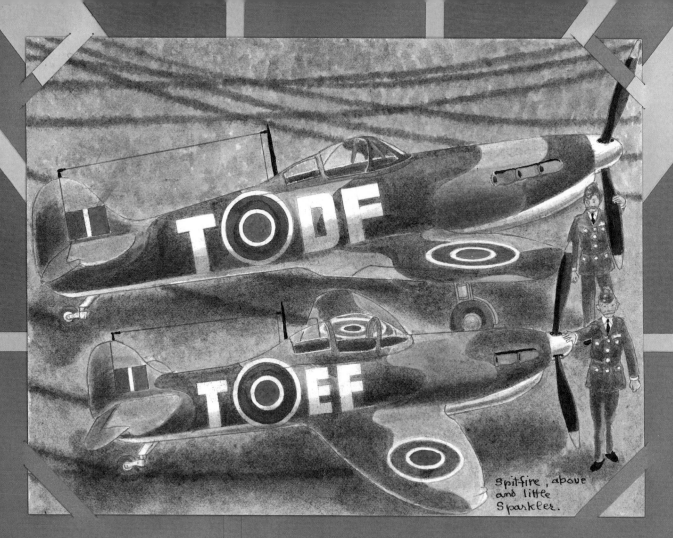

Spitfire, above
and little
Sparkler.

To the King...
and Bayard!

assortment of bright and noisy fireworks was attached to the planes. There were smoke bombs, Bengal lights, Catherine wheels, Roman candles, skyrockets—all these could be electronically set off to make the Sparklers look as though they had been hit and were falling in flames. And while the Teddy-Bear Six would be crash-landing their "burning" planes, their six teddy bears would be seen bailing out and parachuting down to earth.

The six bears were issued parachutes one-third normal size, used for dropping supplies. They were outfitted as RAF pilots and weighted down so that their parachutes would be certain to open.

Commander Carstairs came by to see the Teddy-Bear Six off on their mission. "Gentlemen," said he, "when I first met you and saw your teddy bears, I never dreamed that one day all twelve of you would be suited up and flying off in toy planes to risk all for England. I'm giving you seventeen minutes to get to target and take your pictures, then I'm taking up a backup squadron of twelve real Spit-fires to escort you to the wheat fields. Best of luck, good shooting, and happy crash-landings!" He saluted his men. "See you soon!"

The Teddy-Bear Six took off in tight formation, led by Captain Billy Browne-Browne. Now that the chips were down, the Sparklers seemed unbelievably slow. As predicted by Commander Carstairs, they were near target in fourteen long minutes—three minutes to shoot pictures and straggle home. As predicted by Captain Billy Browne-Browne, the enemy was holding fire, waiting for what it thought to be six real Spitfires to come within range. The enemy was thoroughly fooled—not one antiaircraft burst fouled the clear blue sky.

Pictures taken, the Teddy-Bear Six headed for home. Halfway across the English Channel came the terrifying roar of twelve

Bayard strafed by machine-gun fire

Messerschmitt 262 fighter planes descending on them like a pack of jaguars after a flock of sheep. Then dead ahead loomed Commander Carstairs and his Spitfire squadron. The German planes refused to give up the chase.

The Teddy-Bear Six, in their tiny, unarmed, slow Sparklers, found themselves smack in the middle of a thundering dogfight. Commander Carstairs tried to lure the Messerschmitts away, but they were intent on hunting Sparklers. The Teddy-Bear Six just made it over land, and almost simultaneously their six airplanes appeared to burst into multicolored smoke and flames. Seeing what looked to be six British pilots descending in parachutes, the Messerschmitts turned and flew directly into the blazing cross fire of Commander Carstairs's Spitfires. The Germans lost four planes before roaring back to their base.

Being in charge of the Teddy-Bear Six mission, Captain Billy Browne-Browne had acted as decoy, lagged behind his men, and was the last to set off his fireworks and bail out his bear. With the film left in his camera, he even dared to risk photographing Bayard Bear in the sky. To his horror, he saw Bayard strafed by machine-gun fire, one bullet cleanly removing his left ear and another nicking a chunk out of his left arm. The Teddy-Bear Six, to a man, crash-landed safely in wheat fields, and Commander Carstairs's squadron flew back to base, safe and sound.

As the only casualty, Bayard Bear, after being praised, consoled, and properly bandaged, was given a shelf of honor over the bar in the Officers' Club. Thereafter, Bayard was toasted every night, just after the King.

He would have to wait until the war was won to be taken to the Saint Francis Teddy Bear Clinic on Royal Avenue, in London, for a new left ear and a patched left arm.

For taking the first intelligence pictures of the sinister and deadly V-1 "Doodlebug" flying bomb ramps, each of the Teddy-Bear Six was decorated. The extra bit of film showing Bayard Bear parachuting and being strafed by Messerschmitts found its way into newsreels, worldwide.

The second day of June 1953 was a day Billy Browne-Browne will never forget. It was his fifteenth wedding anniversary, which coincided with the day Elizabeth of Windsor was crowned Queen Elizabeth II of England, and it was the day Bayard Bear was kidnapped.

Three generations of Browne-Brownes were invited to the Coronation Ball: Lord Malcolm and Lady Irma; Lord Peter and Lady Betty; and Lord Billy himself and Lady Avis. That fateful day, they were to meet first at Billy's for drinks before driving to Prunier's for a lobster and champagne Anniversary Dinner, then on to the ball at Buckingham Palace.

Billy well remembered dressing Bayard. It had been so difficult doing up his starched shirt with tiny pearl studs and gold cuff links. He seemed to remember taking him down to the car. Fitting six people, ladies in ball gowns and gentlemen in top hats, in a Jaguar took some thinking. He remembered tucking in hems of long dresses before the leather-lined doors closed by themselves with a pleasant "callumph" sound.

At Prunier's, the doorman was in the process of helping Lady Irma out of the back seat when Billy let out a piercing shriek: "WHERE'S

BAYARD!" He proceeded to drag his parents out, emptying the car, then dove head-first under the dashboard, then dove over the front seats, under the rear seats, then back again over the front seats, under the steering wheel, running both hands back and forth through the red carpet and rubber footpads. Sir Malcolm, with a great impatience which came with his eighty-seven years of age, shouted, "You simply didn't bring him!" He was host of the dinner party. He had chosen what he thought to be the only decent restaurant near the Palace and was dying to get at his lobster.

"I'm going home to get him!" Billy snapped back.

"You young fool!" exclaimed Sir Malcolm. "Bayard doesn't even have an invitation!"

"Bayard doesn't need one!" said Billy, roaring off with screeching tires.

He returned three-quarters of an hour later, white as a ghost. "Bayard's gone, gone, gone!" he muttered.

"He'll show up, darling," Lady Avis said, putting her arms around him. "I know he will. He's never been lost."

Billy shrugged her off. "I've searched the house top to bottom, Bayard's gone!"

"Eat your lobster," his father said.

"I can't."

"Then drink your champagne!" Sir Malcolm commanded.

He didn't need to be told that; he was downing it glass after glass.

They arrived at Buckingham Palace at precisely the minute and hour requested. Getting in line with other Lords and Ladies, they presented their respect, love, and admiration for their Queen, who in turn had a thoughtful word for each of her subjects. As Sir Billy bowed, Her Majesty smiled sweetly and asked, "Where's Bayard?" Seeing him turn pale and start to shake all over, she quickly turned to greet the next Lord and Lady in line.

Billy was shattered. His Queen had asked after his bear, who had been expected and wasn't there. He was perhaps gone forever!

Billy reeled around the Palace ballroom in a trance, tears in his eyes, bumping into people, knocking off their coronets and tiaras . . . Suddenly Commander Carstairs came rushing up to him. He grabbed Billy by the arms: "Steady, man, steady!"

"You!" Sir Billy shouted. "You're just the man I've got to see!"

"Then see me at the Yard at ten tomorrow morning. I'm terribly busy now." He left, and Billy seemed to calm down a bit.

After the war, Commander Carstairs had returned to Scotland Yard to resume his position as inspector. He was at the Coronation Ball to keep a close eye on the Crown Jewels—still protecting "Sparklers," as it were.

Returning home after a disastrous evening, Billy again combed his house, attic to cellar. No Bayard. The next morning, he was at Scotland Yard at nine-thirty, pacing up and down outside Commander Carstairs's office.

At ten minutes to ten, an assistant called him over and told him to please be seated. "Inspector Carstairs phoned to say he was coming right over and to start filling in the forms. What is the nature of your problem?"

"A kidnapping."

The assistant was a cool chap, unabashed by theft or murder. He filled in a crime report as dispassionately as one might make a laundry list.

"Name?"

"His name is Bayard."

"Your son?"

"Bayard's more than a son to me."

"Color of hair?"

"Honey brown."

"Eyes?"

"Sepia jet."

"What was he wearing?"

"Full dress suit and top hat."

"Height?"

"Twenty-two inches."

"Age?"

"Thirty-two years old last May . . . Oh, here's Carstairs." He stood to greet his former commander.

Carstairs's assistant took the inspector aside and whispered a few words to him, then opened a door.

"Come into my office, Captain Billy," said Inspector Carstairs. "This is dreadful. Am I to understand that your Bayard, our dear old friend and RAF hero, has been kidnapped?"

Billy nodded, then covered a tragic face with both hands.

"I'm sorry, frightfully sorry, indeed." He studied some mail on his desk. "May I suggest that you try the Lost Property Office, 200 Baker Street. That would seem to be the appropriate place to look for him. Look here, I have a good friend there. I'll call him at once—"

"My Bayard has been *kidnapped*!"

"This is going to sound cruel," Inspector Carstairs said, "very cruel, to say the least. The daily business of Scotland Yard involves sadistic murder, international drug smuggling, political assassination, million-pound bank embezzlements . . . How much would you say a thirty-two-year-old teddy bear would be worth—ten shillings?"

Sir Billy Browne-Browne stood straight as a ramrod, saluted Inspector Carstairs, did a military about-face, and marched out of the office, slamming the door behind him.

)56

He wandered off aimlessly in great distress. "Even the police won't help me!" he screamed. Then, seeing people staring at him, he jumped into a cab and gave his home address. Nearing his house, he thought, "Maybe there'll be news of Bayard."

There was news of Bayard. He found a rectangular package leaning against his front door. He took it inside, ripped it open, and found Bayard's dress suit, top hat, shirt, underclothing, socks, and shoes—everything except for the bear himself, his pearl studs and gold cuff links. There was a note made of letters scissored out of a newspaper and glued to a piece of wrapping paper. It read:

HAVE BEAR. IF YOU WANT HIM
MEET ME IN CROUDED PLACE
THE TIMES
BETWEEN 4 & 7
BRING £500 IN ALLIGATOR CASE

This sordid ransom note brought a ray of hope to Billy. He put the package under his arm and ran for help to the house of the member of the Teddy-Bear Six living nearest to him. The other members were summoned at once. In an atmosphere of fraternal condolence, the case was reviewed, start to finish, with a seriousness—at long last —befitting the tragedy.

The ransom note was their biggest clue to the crime. They each took a different colored pencil. They passed the note around, marking it as they discussed it, thought by thought.

"Looks to be the work of a ruffian," said one member. "See the way he spells CROUDED with a U where there should be a W." He drew a circle around the word.

"Of course," said another, "the whole message is positively illiterate."

HAVe BeAR. If you want hiM meet Me in Crouded plACe

THE TIMES

BeTWeen **4** & 7 ?!

BRing £500 in aLLigatoR CaSe

"I don't think he knows what you look like," one said. "The alligator case must be so he can pick you out of the crowd."

"What's *The Times* doing in the middle of it all?"

"Hold on here, the letters seem to have been cut from *The Times*."

"That's true."

"Perhaps the rascal means that you are to place an announcement in the Personal Columns of *The Times* stating the hour, day, and place you're to meet."

"Right."

"Wait a minute! I can't picture ruffians reading *The Times* . . ."

"And 'between 4 & 7.' I think this 'ruffian' is a child!"

"He wants to meet you on his way home from school . . ."

"And he wants to meet you in a crowded place, thinking a gentleman wouldn't dare beat up a child in front of a crowd."

"I wouldn't bet my money on that," Billy mumbled.

After great thought and consultation, the Teddy-Bear Six composed an invitation which they telephoned in to *The Times*:

> CHILDREN! You are all invited to a Teddy Bear Costume Ball, between 4 & 7, Saturday afternoon, June 9, at the Grand Ballroom of the Savoy Hotel. A £500 prize will be given to the child wearing the best costume. You must have a teddy bear with you to get in. Otherwise, admission is free.

In all, fifty-two children came to the party. Two members of the Teddy-Bear Six stationed themselves in the cloakroom, where all teddy bears were checked as the children entered. Billy was to be told the minute Bayard arrived. His bear would be identified by the machine-gun scar on his left arm. Billy and the three others wandered nervously on the outskirts of the dance floor, sipping a pink, overly sweet fruit punch with fresh strawberries floating on top. In the first half hour, more than thirty children arrived—little sheiks, nurses, shepherdesses, Pierrots, Pierrettes, ghosts, cowboys, Zulus. They were laughing and screaming and pelting Billy and his friends with confetti, cotton balls, and paper serpentines. A tiny clown took his false nose off and gave it to Sir Billy. "You look sad," said he.

There was no news of Bayard.

"What if our famous 'ruffian' is a grown man?" Billy asked.

"Then we're six bigger fools than we already appear to be."

Carroll Gibbons's Orchestra played a carefully selected program of Cole Porter, Rodgers and Hart, and Noël Coward tunes, with "The Teddy Bear's Picnic" sandwiched in every six numbers. Ice cream and cake weighed down every table. The noise in the ballroom was close to infernal when the fat member of the Teddy-Bear Six rushed up to Sir Billy. "He's arrived, *Bayard's here!*" The two rushed off to the cloakroom. "He's up there, number 41. At first the boy didn't want to check him. He said he wanted to see 'the man with the alligator case' directly. I told him to join the party and that he'd be certain to get his prize 'in a *crouded* place,' as he himself had specified. He handed me Bayard, then had the nerve to say that I looked somewhat honest."

Sir Billy was too busy hugging and mumbling sentimental mush to Bayard to pay much attention. He checked him over top to bottom and found him to be safe and sound. He replaced Bayard in slot 41 on a top shelf. "I think he'll be quite safe here," he said, "but we must take turns guarding him."

"Of course. I'll stay here. Go on back and meet the kidnapper."

He joined the other four members of the Teddy-Bear Six, who were deep in serious discussion. "What's up?" Sir Billy asked.

"We were wondering whether, without possibly seeming to cheat, we could award the prize for the best costume to the kidnapper."

"Good Lord, where is he?" Sir Billy asked nervously.

"He's the purple pirate over there."

Sir Billy looked and saw a scrappy-looking chap jumping up and down, making far more noise than the other children, and from time to time swatting little girls' backsides with a rubber cutlass. "His attitude is quite swashbuckling, one might say. Part of a good costume is how well one wears it."

"We've analyzed his costume. We guess that he comes from a large and poor family. The boots and belt appear to be his. We think he's wearing his grandmother's purple knickers. The shirt is probably his older sister's nightshirt. He has cleverly tied his hatcheck disk around his neck with a ribbon, like a Spanish doubloon. His eye patch and the burnt-cork makeup smeared all over his face are to hide his identity. The skull-and-crossbones is hand-painted."

"I vote the prize for the Purple Pirate," Sir Billy mumbled.

"And we do, too!"

A drumroll silenced the children, who were told to form a large circle on the edge of the dance floor. A small tall table was placed in the center, with an alligator attaché case on top of it. It was clicked open. Inside were neat stacks of five-pound notes tied up with green silk ribbons. There was a loud gasp—then silence.

A member of the Teddy-Bear Six stepped forward, stood behind the alligator case, and took from his pocket scraps of paper, which he examined and seemed to count. "By six votes to nil, the jury has declared the Purple Pirate winner of the prize for best costume!"

There was applause, hesitant at first, then quite unanimous. The Purple Pirate hadn't exactly passed unnoticed. No one seemed to disapprove.

He was nowhere to be seen.

"Don't be shy, dear Pirate," the announcer said. "Step up, collect your prize, and simply walk away with it. After this, you all must leave. It is past seven o'clock and the party is over. The ballroom must be tidied up for another party."

A cowboy and a sheik first turned, then separated, making room for the Purple Pirate, whose behavior had turned discreet. He hadn't tried to hide before. He seemed to move in slow motion. His eyes looked all about him but avoided the prize. His boots seemed stuck to the dance floor, as in a molasses dream. He never got close enough to the alligator case to reach for the money. He stopped short, much too far away from it, and reached out a hand that trembled like a leaf. Then the Purple Pirate burst into tears, shrieked, and bolted empty-handed from the ballroom.

"Fancy that," said Sir Billy Browne-Browne. "Children, thank you so much for coming. Have a lovely evening."

The Teddy-Bear Six didn't need a better excuse for yet another bash. They ran from the Savoy, crossed the Strand, and burst into Rule's on Maiden Lane. Bayard Bear sat at the head of the table, wearing just a napkin tied around his neck. He was toasted twenty-one times, like the Queen on her birthday.

Two days later, Sir Billy received a tiny package containing Bayard's pearl studs and gold cuff links and a handwritten note:

> *Dear Sir,*
>
> *You sat your bear on top of your car the night of the Coronation. You then stuffed your family inside the car and drove off, forgetting him. He bounced off in the street, and I got him. Seeing how grandly he was dressed, I thought first of a reward, then a ransom. I'm terribly sorry I did it!*
>
> *Thank you so much for the party. It was SMASHING!*

63(

1967

Sir Billy Browne-Browne's marriage to Lady Avis was a happy one. They had two pretty girls, two years apart, and took enormous joy in bringing them up. Alexandra had strawberry-blond hair and emerald eyes. She took life seriously. She tended to be strict with her sister, who she thought was somewhat giddy. Valérie's hair was ash-blond, her eyes were lavender, and she was rarely without a sly grin on her face.

Her mother once told Valérie that people never knew what she was thinking when she smiled at them. "I know," she said, but as I'm usually not thinking much of anything, my smile lends a curiously incisive edge to my lack of intellect."

"Oh, shut up, Valérie!" Alexandra said.

"Yes, dear," said Valérie, smiling.

Children have a way of steering a different course than that chosen by their parents. Alexandra and Valérie talked a lot. They demanded telephones, one each, which caused an upheaval in the household. The girls' rooms were moved to the top floor, out of the way. There, each sister on her own bed, propped with pillows, talked, talked, and talked, a babble of badinage which their father once described as "useless noise more expensive than the London Philharmonic Orchestra."

Bayard Bear held a great fascination for the sisters. This started when they were young and small and Bayard was placed above them, out of reach. Owners are terribly nervous about their teddy bears being touched by others. Children can be rough with bears, and much touching wears away the fur. This was to be seen, ever so sadly, one afternoon at a racetrack.

Sir Billy and Bayard went to sports events everywhere. They could be seen in the Browne-Browne family box at Wimbledon, at the Grand National Steeplechase at Aintree, at the Henley Royal Regatta, at cricket test matches—they were not talkers but watchers.

One night, a dapper young man—no friend of Billy's—had an incredible dream in which he ran into Lord Browne-Browne and Bayard Bear at a racetrack. He touched the teddy bear's head between the ears, then bet 580 pounds on a horse named Panda's Wine Cork.

The fellow was mystified by the dream because he never bet on horses. He kept some cash in a box in his house, which both he and his wife used as needed. Out of curiosity, he counted what was there. It came to exactly 580 pounds. In his dream, Bayard was wearing a pearl-gray top hat. This meant the race must be the Ascot Stakes. That gala race was to be run that afternoon. He looked in his newspaper and found that Panda's Wine Cork was running in the Stakes, listed as an outsider. He drove full speed to Ascot, found Sir Billy and Bayard there, touched Bayard's head, and bet all of his 580 pounds.

The next day, *The Daily Express* had a front-page picture of the chap with the headline: TOUCHES BAYARD'S HEAD—WINS £13,380!

65(

Billy and Bayard went to the racetrack just once after that. It was a terrifying experience. They had no sooner gone through the gate to the grounds than someone shouted, "Bayard's here!" Lord Billy Browne-Browne and Bayard Bear, both of whom hated close contact with people, found themselves mobbed like rock stars. It took a platoon of the track police to rescue them. Bayard's head had been rubbed by so many greedy bettors he had a bald spot between the ears.

Sitting at home that evening, red with anger, Billy received a cable from America which read: "Always knew Bayard was magic. Can't wait to get in touch with him. Been transferred to Chicago, a giant step closer to our interview." It was signed Richard Marshall. Billy crumpled it up and threw it away.

Being constantly in the news, Bayard received a lot of mail and quite a few presents from total strangers. When Alexandra and Valérie were young, just learning to read, what interested them most were Bayard's letters. How could such a small chap be so admired? In 1967, when Alexandra was eighteen and Valérie sixteen, Bayard Bear had become so famous he needed assistants to answer his fan mail. The girls handled this job with considerable tact and wit, Alexandra answering the serious letters, and Valérie the funny ones.

In 1970, to celebrate the twenty-fifth anniversary of the end of World War II, *The Times* sent out as Christmas cards five thousand quarter-sized copies of the 1945 issue announcing the Allied victory. One thousand seven hundred and thirty-nine of these were forwarded to Bayard Bear. He had fought the war, and these newspapers seemed to have been printed just for him. The girls sent out thank-you notes.

Somewhere around that time, the Brewster Coachwork Company, designers and manufacturers of distinguished bodies for motorcars

In a matter of seconds, Sir Billy was the center of a nightmare of strangers' hands, all trying to touch Bayard Bear!

which were "Guaranteed to outlast the chassis," went out of business. People no longer cared how long a car would last—they changed them every year. Brewster sent Bayard an extraordinary model of a 1931 Rolls-Royce Croydon Coupé. "We believe this fine model to be just the right size for Bayard. We cannot think of a more suitable gentleman to be its owner. We present it to him with our compliments and hope that he will find it to his liking." Bayard Bear spent two nights in it, sitting behind the steering wheel. Alexandra and Valérie then removed him and polished the car, end to end, with jeweler's rouge.

Bayard received foreign hats. When men still bought hats, hatmakers sometimes displayed small models of their wares in their windows. These little hats seemed to have made a great many travelers think of Bayard. He received a bullfighter's hat from Spain, a policeman's hat from Paris, a ten-gallon hat from Texas, a straw gondolier's hat from Venice, and even a Napoleon Bonaparte hat from Corsica. Valérie loved to answer hat letters. She never wrote in them that bears hardly ever wear hats. Their ears get in the way.

Sir Robert Kenneth Duncan, of the architectural firm of Duncan & Lucas, sent Bayard a scale model of the four-story London town house he had designed and built for the Browne-Brownes. This model house opened up as a wardrobe for Bayard Bear's suits. The top floor was labeled Spring, the third floor Summer, the second floor Autumn, and the ground floor Winter.

Alexandra and Valérie sorted out Bayard's extensive wardrobe, seeing that his suits were cleaned, pressed, and hung in seasonal order.

There was one aspect to the girls' work which never failed to make their father fume. About once or twice a month, a much loved and worn teddy bear would be mailed to him. These were accompanied by letters which were practically all the same:

Dear Lord Browne-Browne,

My son Tommy is seven years old and feels that he is a bit old for Bumpsy, his teddy bear. He cannot imagine throwing him in the trash can and we thought you would be the right person to see that the remainder of Bumpsy's life is made cozy and comfortable. We know that he will be an excellent friend and companion for Bayard, and . . .

The girls forwarded these bears to orphanages and children's hospitals, where teddy bears are always needed.

"I don't run an Old Bears' Home!" Billy would mumble.

His incredible speech
lasted one full minute
and forty-one seconds
without a single word
being spoken

To the sound of
thunderous
applause,
Sir Billy turned
beet-red

1975

Sir Billy Browne-Browne and Bayard Bear spent a great deal of their time in the House of Lords. They sat in the first of the crossbenches, so that Bayard would be in plain sight. In 1975, Sir Billy was speaking less than ever. When a bill came up for debate, Bayard was dressed to state Sir Billy's opinion. It was a simple color code based on logic and tradition. A white suit meant: "Do whatever you like. I couldn't care less." A brown suit meant: "Dullest proposal ever made!" A red suit meant: "Over my dead body!" A kilt meant: "Too damned expensive!" A green suit meant: "Hear! Hear!" A wedding suit meant: "I do, too." An orange suit meant: "Proceed with caution." A yellow suit meant: "I'm much afraid of the whole idea." And a blue suit meant: "A sad day for England!"

During one Second Reading debate, Bayard Bear was sitting on top of the crossbench. He was wearing an orange suit. This infuriated the loud and formidable Lord Lester Beachwood.

Lord Beachwood stood up, clenched his fists, swelled his chest, and aimed his booming voice at Lord Billy, who was about to doze off in deep, absentminded contentment. "It is a known fact to all of us that every time Lord Browne-Browne has a suit made, his tailor makes the same suit for Bayard Bear. Now wouldn't it be simpler—perhaps more dignified—if Lord Billy were to leave Bayard in the clothes closet and he himself take out the suit which goes with his opinion? I cannot help but think that the jumbo-sized orange suit made to envelop his ample girth would go a long way towards making the House of Lords a gayer place in which to breathe."

There was a beginning of laughter, cut short when Lord Billy Browne-Browne sprang up. This brought total silence. What would the man who rarely spoke have to say?

He made an incredible wordless reply ranging from fury, to indignation, to tenderness for Bayard and total mockery of the bombastic Lord Beachwood. This lasted one full minute and forty-one seconds. The Lords, standing up as a man, cheered and applauded him seven and a half minutes. Lord Billy Browne-Browne had flailed his arms about, picked up Bayard, displayed him to all present, held him in his arms, aped Lord Lester Beachwood, bowed triumphantly, and sat down. He hadn't uttered a single word.

It was a brilliant exercise in silence.

Every newspaper in London praised the return of true eloquence to the House of Lords. Sir Billy Browne-Browne was compared most favorably with William Pitt, Benjamin Disraeli, and Lloyd George. *The Observer* suggested, editorially, that if other public figures had the good taste to follow Sir Billy's example, "the air of fair England would be far less polluted."

The Indian member of the Teddy-Bear Six, feeling that Billy's and Bayard's feelings might have been ruffled, held a Teddy-Bear Six bash at his London home. It was the sixty-seventh of these affairs, and possibly the warmest. The curry served was so hot it took two dozen bottles of Dom Pérignon to soothe flaming throats.

The next afternoon Billy received another cable from America: "Everything I hear about you and Bayard leaves me speechless, too. I've been transferred again, this time to New York. I'm just an ocean hop away from an interview. How about it?" It was signed Richard Marshall.

"I hope he doesn't get his feet wet," Billy told Bayard, handing the cable to Alexandra and Valérie. "Girls, you may file this in the wastebasket."

"I'd just as soon not speak to you."

"I'd like a game of billiards."

"Keep the whiskies coming."

1985

When Lord Billy Browne-Browne was at his London club, Bayard Bear's suits again did most of the talking. When Bayard wore a red suit, it meant that Billy would just as soon not talk to anyone. If he wore a green suit, it meant that Billy would like a game of billiards. If the bear wore a Scottish kilt, it simply meant that the club steward was to keep the whiskies coming.

This crystal-clear set of signals had no effect on Richard Marshall, who had flown in from New York that very day to interview Sir Billy.

And Bayard Bear was wearing his red suit!

"He's come a long way, sir," the club steward offered ever so timidly. "He says it will just take five minutes."

Sir Billy turned his head for a quick look at the insolent chap. He was standing in the doorway, smiling and nodding. He was neatly dressed in a shapeless suit. "Good God!" Sir Billy thought. "He must be that American chap who sends cables." He looked up at the steward. "I'll answer two questions."

The steward went up to the man. "Just two questions, sir," he said.

The fellow paused for thought, straightened his tie, and bravely approached Sir Billy. "I'm Richard Marshall—"

"I know, what's your first question?"

"I guess it's this: What has spending a lifetime with Bayard Bear brought you?"

"Well," said Sir Billy, "I think that what you really mean is this: What, other than making me seem a perfect fool, has spending a lifetime with Bayard brought me? I'll tell you what. Bayard has constantly looked after my best interests. He taught me how to walk downstairs. He saw me through hard times at school. He outjumped me, and anybody since, in the 1936 Olympic Games. He saved me from shaking hands with Adolf Hitler. He found an adorable wife for me. He acted as decoy for me during a tight war situation. He saved me from making speeches in the House of Lords and, to sum it up, he's always been the greatest companion, an affable chap of great comfort to me, and he doesn't even mind keeping bores from bothering me in this very club. He's my best friend. What's your last question?"

Richard Marshall seemed to hesitate, as if he knew he was about to ask something shattering. "Sir Billy," he ventured, "from all appearances you seem to lead a comfortable life. Yet you have no real profession, and with taxes what they are in Britain, how can you possibly make ends meet?" He quickly ducked back as though warding off a punch in the nose.

Sir Billy Browne-Browne's red face turned pale. He pointed a waving finger near the interviewer's head and shouted, "You must have been born impudent!"

A dozen other members of the club, who were discreetly slumped in easy chairs, dropped their newspapers.

Shaking, and glaring at Richard Marshall, Lord Billy Browne-Browne continued. "I promised you two questions and I'll jolly well give you two answers. Even you," said he, "have heard of the stately homes of England. They are estates so vast not even a millionaire could afford to keep them. We are obliged to have guided tours on given days, for which visitors pay a fee. Well, thanks to Bayard Bear, ours is by far the most popular house in all of England.

"Had it not been for Bayard Bear," he continued, "it would be just another ordinary stately home. How many east wings, west wings, main halls, solariums, bad family portraits, can any visitor take in? Ours is unusual to start with, with Lady Avis's Olympic swimming pool and diving platforms, neatly hidden by three-hundred-year-old oak trees, lending an anachronistic touch. There are rather special little rooms, small museums. There is Lord Malcolm's room, where my grandfather's cricket bats, caps, trophies, and photographs can be seen. There is the tennis room, where Lord Peter and Lady Betty's rackets, cups, trophies, and photographs can be seen. But most popular of all is the Bayard Bear Wing. There are moving pictures on the walls at either end. One wall has the newsreel of his and my Olympic jumps and our bizarre confrontation with Hitler. The other shows the Teddy-Bear Six Sparklers pretending to go down in flames. One can actually see Bayard's ear get nicked off and his dear little arm being wounded. There is a wall papered with *The Times*'s 1970 Christmas card, a quarter-sized issue of the paper which announced the end of the war. There is Bayard's Brewster-bodied Rolls-Royce. It's a great favorite. It's left-hand drive, by the way, designed for the American trade. There is his wardrobe, contained in a model of my London town house. There is a special display of the clothing which marked Bayard Bear's life—his first sailor suit, Hammer School blazer, Olympic Games track suit. There is his RAF pilot uniform, best-man wedding suit—unpressed—and others leading up to his House of Lords robe and wig presented to him by the Queen. I'm always amused by children, because they cannot seem to understand why his sailor suit is the same size as his RAF uniform. Bayard is so real to them they feel he must have done some growing some time.

"Then the RAF has lent us a little Sparkler fighter plane, used in the photographing raid. Children love to climb all over it. And his parachute is there, riddled with bullet holes.

"There is a glass showcase of mementos of Bayard's kidnapping. The Scotland Yard crime report is on display, along with the rectangular package with evening clothes and top hat, the ransom note, the winning cloakroom disks, number 41, are both there, as is the small box with pearl studs and gold cuff links, the young kidnapper's letter, all there—everything sprinkled with confetti and cotton balls.

"The place is jammed whenever we open it to the public. Visiting days are indeed very long. When such a day is over, after the last visitor has left, Lady Avis is in the pantry making bread and honey, while I sit in the parlor, counting all the money. Bayard supports every one of us in grand style, God bless him! Does that answer your question?"

"It certainly does, Sir Billy. It sounds fascinating! I can hardly wait to go—"

"What's keeping you?" asked Lord Billy Browne-Browne, leaping to his feet. He smiled privately, shook hands with his interviewer, and bid him farewell.

He sunk back down deep in his chair. "Bayard, please be a good chap and don't speak to me. I've never talked so much in my whole life!"